RORY AND HIS SECRET VOYAGE

Author: Andrew Wolffe   Illustrator: Tom Cole

This edition published 2000   ISBN: 0 9534949 4 2

A CIP catalogue record for this book is available from the British Library.

Printed in Singapore

Keppel Publishing Ltd
The Grey House, Kenbridge Road,
New Galloway, DG7 3RP, Scotland

Includes free RORY STORIES character to cut out and collect.

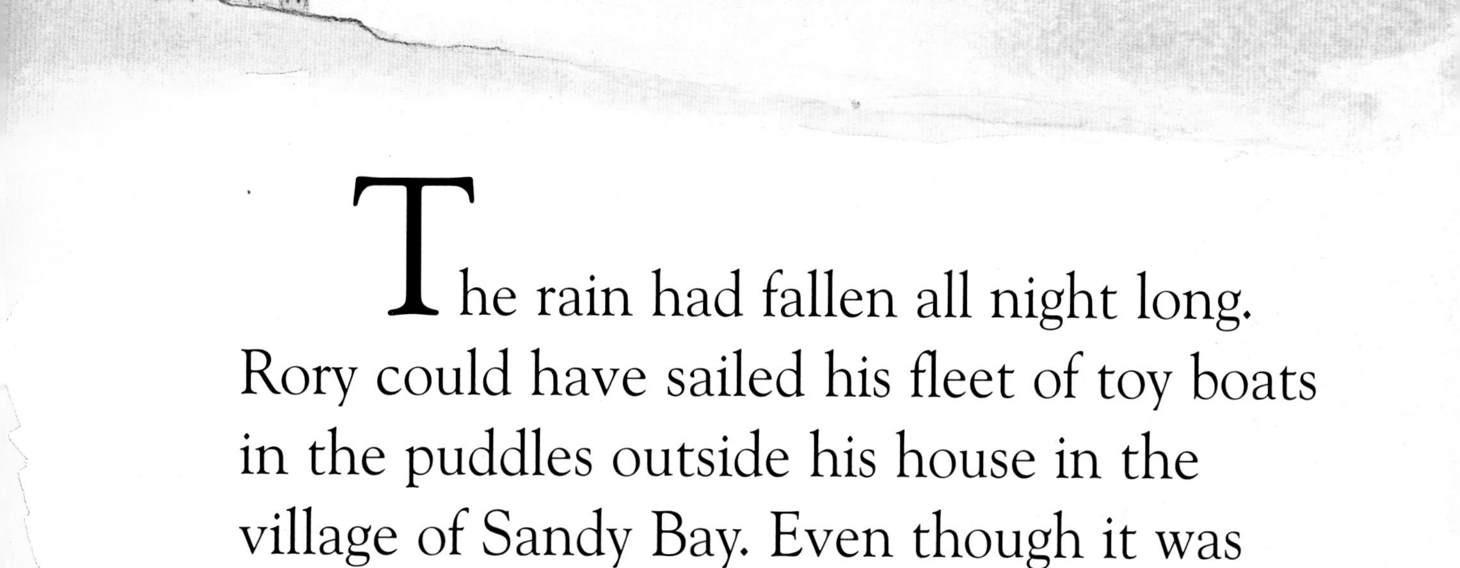

The rain had fallen all night long. Rory could have sailed his fleet of toy boats in the puddles outside his house in the village of Sandy Bay. Even though it was morning, the sky was still full of dark clouds and it looked as if the rain would never stop.

"I don't think we'll be able to go down to the beach today," Rory said sadly to his little dog, Scruff McDuff, as they both finished breakfast.

"Why don't you come with me to work?" suggested Rory's Dad. "You and Scruff McDuff will find plenty to keep you busy at the boat yard."

Sandy Bay Boat Yard has been in Rory's family for as long as anyone in the village can remember. Rory's great grandfather started the yard and now Rory's Dad looks after it.

Boats of all shapes and sizes are repaired in the yard. As well as giving old boats another lease of life, Rory's Dad builds new boats. Some are sleek, some are fast, some are curved, some are very special, but all of them always look wonderful.

Rory and Scruff McDuff love visiting the boat yard. There's a massive crane that lifts boats in and out of the water and a stone slipway that's used to launch boats. One of their favourite games is to explore the huge sheds, where parts of old boats and forgotten treasures from long-ago voyages to far-away lands are stacked in every nook and cranny.

"Don't get up to too much mischief," warned Rory's Dad as he climbed the stairs to his office.

"We won't," promised Rory, while Scruff McDuff looked suitably serious.

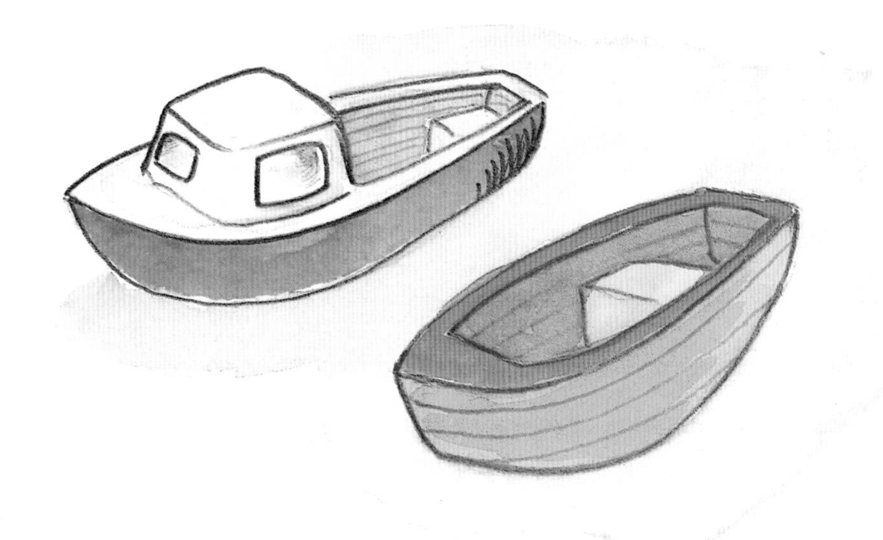

Rory and Scruff McDuff ran quickly to the nearest shed. “Let’s go in here,” Rory suggested just in time for them to miss another heavy downpour of rain. “We haven’t had a good look in here before and I want to see an old boat that Dad told me about.”

Even though there were no doors across the entrance, the inside of the shed was quite dark. Rory and Scruff McDuff had to wait a moment or two until their eyes got used to the dim light before going any further.

"Look," exclaimed Rory suddenly, making Scruff McDuff jump. "Right at the back of the shed. Can you see it?" he added, pointing to an old abandoned boat.

"Dad told me that it was the best of its kind when it was built," Rory said, spotting a wooden gangway. "We can go on board, Dad said it's safe."

Slowly and carefully, Rory and Scruff McDuff made their way up the gangway and on to the deck of the boat. Everything that had been used on the boat's last voyage was still there and exactly where it should have been, except that it was all covered in cobwebs.

"Dad says he's going to repair the boat one of these days," Rory told Scruff McDuff who was sniffing at a gigantic spider sleeping in a coiled rope. "Let's explore down below," said Rory as he pushed open one of the doors with a loud and spooky CREAK!

Soon Rory and Scruff McDuff were in an old cabin that had eight windows, four on either side of the room. "They're called portholes," Rory explained. "But windows on boats are supposed to be round and these aren't, I wonder why?" he said, pointing at the oddly shaped windows.

Rory climbed up on to the seat and looked out of the window shaped like a triangle, expecting to see the inside of the shed. Instead, he saw a magnificent sailing ship being blown across the ocean by the wind.

Rory leaned back from the window and rubbed his eyes. "Maybe I imagined it," he said sensibly. "Let's try another window."

They looked out of the square window. "Fantastic!" cried Rory as he watched a massive liner being launched and slowly slide into the sea, then sail off, full steam ahead.

Next Rory and Scruff McDuff crouched down to look out of the small diamond-shaped window. Much to their amazement they saw a mermaid sitting on top of a rock, brushing her hair and warming her tail in bright sunshine.

Finally, Rory and Scruff McDuff looked out of the window shaped like a flower and saw several old boats racing each other. The boat in front seemed very familiar. “Look,” shouted Rory, “it’s this boat and it’s going to win.” As the boat sailed past the window, Rory spied the captain. “It’s my great grandfather,” he gasped.

When Rory and Scruff McDuff looked out of the window again, they saw Rory's Dad walking up the shed towards the boat.

"Come on you two," he called. "It's time for lunch. I don't know what you've been up to. You can't have seen anything very exciting in that old boat."

But Rory and Scruff McDuff knew better than that.

Cut out and keep Rory and Scruff McDuff to add to your collection of characters from THE RORY STORIES.